The Nut

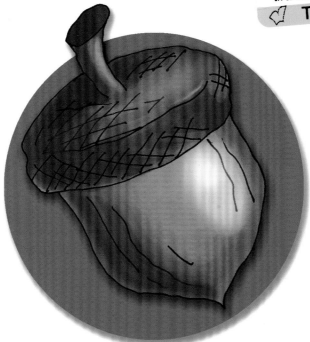

by Susan Hartley • illustrated by Anita DuFalla

The nut is up on the hut in the sun.

Pat cannot see the nut.

Pat can see the nut,
but it is not on the hut.

The pup is in the sun.
The pup is on the nut,
but the pup cannot see it.

Pat can see a cup.

Pat has the cup.

The pup is at the cup.

The pup cannot see Pat.

Pat has the nut.

The nut is up on the hut

in the sun with Pat.